'Everyone in our class excep   pet,' said
Garth mournfully. 'Some of them've got two or
three.'

Poor Garth! Lumbered with a mother who
didn't like dogs (they chewed up the furniture and
wanted walks all the time), didn't care for the courting habits of cats and detested mice and gerbils, as
well as a father who wouldn't have budgies, Garth
was left with only an empty rabbit-hutch and an
imaginary pet crocodile to dream about. Until the
night his father won Victor in a raffle and brought
him home. Not a budgie, chicken or a duck, Victor
was a baby vulture with a merry, knowing expression
and Garth loved him at once. But keeping a growing
vulture in a small garden can have its problems, as
Garth and his family realized when Councillor
Dobbs spotted Victor one day and sparked off a
council enquiry.

The battle that rages over Victor's head and
Garth's determined fight to keep his unusual pet
make irresistible reading for six- to eight-year-
olds.

JANE HOLIDAY

Victor the Vulture

Illustrated by Jo Worth

PUFFIN BOOKS

Puffin Books, Penguin Books Ltd, Harmondsworth, Middlesex, England
Penguin Books, 625 Madison Avenue, New York, New York 10022, U.S.A.
Penguin Books Australia Ltd, Ringwood, Victoria, Australia
Penguin Books Canada Ltd, 2801 John Street, Markham, Ontario, Canada L3R 1B4
Penguin Books (N.Z.) Ltd, 182–190 Wairau Road, Auckland 10, New Zealand

First published by Hamish Hamilton Children's Books Ltd 1978
Published in Puffin Books 1981

Copyright © Jane Holiday, 1978
Illustrations copyright © Jo Worth, 1978
All rights reserved

Made and printed in Great Britain by
Richard Clay (The Chaucer Press) Ltd, Bungay, Suffolk
Set in Monophoto Plantin

Chapter One

'MY PET,' the teacher wrote on the blackboard in her neat handwriting. She was young, ginger-haired and snub-nosed. She wore a short pink skirt and pink-flowered blouse.

Thirty-two boys and girls, sitting in groups of four, copied it down. Garth yawned. What a boring cissy subject, he thought. They were all supposed to write about dear little pussie or doggie. Then they had to draw a picture.

'I hate Composition,' he muttered to Robert. 'We never write about anything interesting.'

'Cardboard porridge,' agreed Robert. 'Look at her.' He jerked Garth's elbow and they looked across at Delia Greenwood. She had a pink face and long fair hair.

She had beautifully copied the title and beautifully underlined it. Now she was writing a beautifully neat essay. She was always praised by Miss Molesley for her neat work. Every week Delia's composition would be among those chosen to be read out. Of course she had already written half a page.

'Garth!' came Miss Molesley's voice across the room. 'Everyone else has started. Haven't you any pets?'

'No,' said Garth, going red.

'Oh,' said Miss Molesley, nonplussed. 'Well . . .' she cast about in her mind for a suitable alternative, 'well, you can always write about an imaginary pet.'

'Yes miss,' said Garth. He thought for a few moments.

'My pet is a crocodile called Constance,' he wrote. 'She lives in the bath. Luckily we have a spare tin bath in the garden shed. She eats sardines and baked beans and, best of all, although it doesn't tell you this in any books about crocodiles, she likes Instant Whip (butterscotch kind). My mother does not like her very much because she says she has a beady look and she would like my Dad to put her in the tin bath so we could have the pink bath to wash in again.'

'Gosh!' said Robert. 'You haven't half written a lot.'

'Ssh,' said Garth. He was busy.

Robert shrugged and went on writing about his gerbil.

Garth was still writing at great speed when Miss Molesley called out, 'All books at the front please. Monitor, collect them and Craig, you collect the

pencils please. Robert Baker! Stop doing that! And Carol, don't suck that dirty glove, dear.'

Garth put up his hand.

Miss Molesley stared at him in surprise. 'Yes Garth?'

'Can I take mine home and finish it?'

Miss Molesley went a pink colour through her biscuity freckles.

'Of course you may, Garth,' she said. 'Don't forget your diary as well. Now children. Stand up. A short prayer before the bell.'

'Whatever did you do that for?' asked Robert a few minutes later as they tore across the playground together. Garth ignored this question and kicked a stone over to him. Robert dribbled gracefully and then kicked it – straight into Delia Greenwood's leg. She looked round. Both boys were walking primly across the playground with their classmates. Delia sniffed. 'All right,' she said. 'I know it was you, Garth Bone, or else you, Robert Baker. Just you wait.'

She ran off angrily, her satchel bobbing up and down on her shoulder.

'Just you wait! Just you wait!' the two boys cried in a high-pitched squawk after her and made clucking sounds like a hen laying eggs.

'Ta-ra,' said Robert at the crossroads. 'Can't play out tonight – we're going to see my auntie.'

Garth walked on, past the old folks' home. He often looked in it as he went by. It was set at the bottom of a slope so that you could see straight in through the huge windows.

Old men and women sat in armchairs lining the walls of a room.

It was all so neat they looked like exhibits in a museum.

'I'll never go in one of those,' he vowed

almost every time he went past. Today he didn't notice them at all. He zigzagged through the pit of sand near the four new houses and the notice saying 'Bodgett and Hickson. Town houses. £6,995' across the grassy patch to the council estate where he lived. Spanking new pebble-dash houses stood in squares; they had long back gardens and beyond these lay a green with newly planted trees.

Garth was lucky. He lived right on the edge of one of the open-ended squares of eight. His house was only a dozen yards from the fields where a few cows and horses dozed in the sun.

A large wooden cage, built by his father, stood at the bottom of the garden. It had been meant as a rabbit-hutch but Garth didn't like rabbits, the only sort of pet his mother seemed willing to tolerate. She didn't like dogs (they chewed up the furniture and wanted walks all the time);

she didn't care for the courting habits of cats; mice and gerbils she detested.

His father did not care for budgies. 'I must be the only one in our class without a pet,' Garth thought morosely. He'd even suggested a hedgehog to his mother but she maintained that they had the greatest number of fleas per square inch of any pet you could name. Garth wondered sometimes how she acquired all this information since she always refused to keep one. He ate his meal moodily that evening. 'What's up, lad?' asked his father while they were eating the delicious shepherd's pie.

'Everyone in our class except me's got a pet,' said Garth. 'Some of them've got two or three.'

Mrs Bone looked worried. 'Most of them are so much trouble to look after,' she said. 'If we have a pet, I should want it looked after properly. It's no good

having a great dog and never taking it for walks, poor thing, like those people down the road. It's bound to get up to mischief then.'

Garth and Mr Bone looked at each other without saying anything. Mrs Bone had never gone so far as to say 'If' before. They both realized they must go warily. Mr Bone winked at his son across the table.

'And you see,' went on Mrs Bone, 'we're all out in the day, except in the holidays.' Mrs Bone was a typist at a local secondary school and Mr Bone was a painter and decorator.

Chapter Two

Garth was asleep when his father came home that evening from his weekly darts night at the 'Red Cat Inn', but woke up at the sound of his parents' voices raised in excited conversation. He crept to the top of the stairs to listen.

'Won it in a raffle!' came his mother's incredulous voice. 'Won it in a raffle?'

'That's right,' said Mr Bone proudly. 'Wicker cage as well.'

'CAGE,' thought Garth. It must be some kind of pet. 'Oh please let me be able to keep it,' he prayed wildly. 'Please. Please.'

'We can't keep it!' cried his mother.

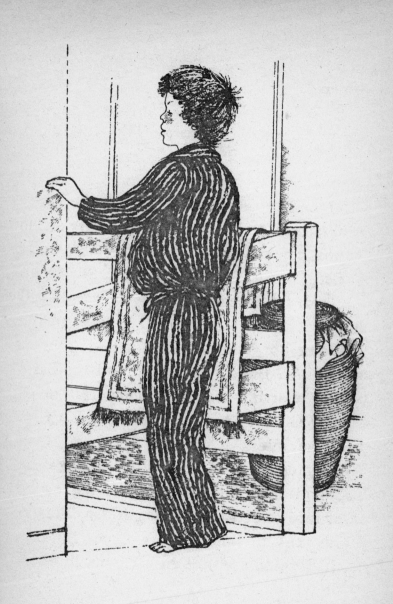

'You can't keep pets in a council house.'

'You what?' said Mr Bone, in complete astonishment. 'You know we can, love. There's everything on this estate from poodles to Pyrenean mountain dogs, not to mention cats, rabbits and gerbils.'

'But you can't keep poultry,' said Mrs Bone.

Garth felt puzzled. Surely it wasn't a hen or a duck?

'Poultry? Vultures aren't poultry,' scoffed Mr Bone.

As Garth crept downstairs on slippered feet (having decided it was time he put a word in), he imagined coming down in the morning to breakfast and his mother saying, 'Now eat your nice boiled vulture's egg, dear.' Or being sent to buy Vulture Chop Suey from the Chinese take-away.

'Well they're certainly not pets,' snapped back his wife.

'No,' conceded Mr Bone. 'But I don't see why not. Lovely looking chap he is. Just look at him.'

Garth looked at the vulture properly then. He knew at once he had made a new friend.

His whole appearance was unusual. His face was a pale plucked question mark above a fluffily brown ruff. He had an oddly shaped brown body with beige feathers in layers. Below this were short sturdy legs and feet. And his expression!

He looked at Garth with a merry, knowing look. They were friends at once.

'Garth!' shouted his mother indignantly. 'Whatever are you doing downstairs? You ought to be in bed.'

Garth ignored this. He looked at the

vulture and then at his parents. 'He's called Victor,' he said. 'I like him. We can keep him, can't we? We can always keep him in the rabbit cage when he gets bigger.'

'Bigger?' gasped Mrs Bone, taking another look at Victor.

'He's right, you know,' said Mr Bone admiringly. 'The lad's right. He's only a baby really.'

Mrs Bone hummed and hawed and finally agreed to give Victor at least a trial period to see how he turned out.

'And since he's only young, love,' said Mr Bone, 'I daresay you can train him up just like a puppy or suchlike.'

Mrs Bone sniffed. 'Him!' she said. 'I daresay you're none too sure he is a he either.'

'Anyway,' said Mr Bone, 'I reckon he'll be all right for tonight. So you be getting back to bed, lad, and we'll put him outside come morning.'

Garth went to bed, tired but very happy. He fell asleep almost at once.

Chapter Three

In the morning, he simply leapt down-stairs, eager for his first sight of Victor.

His father was already up. He was looking worriedly in the fridge for something for Victor to eat. 'He'll not like fish fingers nor butterscotch blancmange.'

'There's a raw chicken,' said Garth hopefully. 'It's not frozen.'

He was surprised when his father seized on it with alacrity.

'Just the job,' he said. 'I daresay he's a tidy eater.'

Garth carried the wicker cage out into

the garden. He undid the clasp and the bird hopped out, blinking a little with bright eyes. Garth scratched his bony head with a twig. The vulture flapped brown wings and stared at him.

As he devoured eagerly the chicken legs Mr Bone gave him, Garth went in to find a bowl for water. The vulture flapped eagerly, bending low his small head, set on a bare, scraped-looking neck. Then he looked up expectantly.

'Darn me if it don't want some more,' said Mr Bone. He went back into the kitchen and returned with the wings which Victor disposed of in an instant.

'Well,' said his father resignedly, 'it might as well have the rest.' Garth watched in amazement as his father prepared to take the rest of the chicken carcase out of the fridge. 'Cardboard porridge!' he said in an awed whisper. 'What will Mum say?'

A furious squawk from Mrs Bone, followed by a long tirade during which she put the chicken carcase back in the fridge, left him in no doubt. She said that if they wanted to give their Sunday dinner to Victor, that was O.K. by her. They could always have sardines. But let them tell her in advance next time. And was that bird going to eat a chicken every day, and if so, she wanted at least an extra £60 a month housekeeping money. Furthermore, he was only a young one, wasn't he, so they'd probably given him far too much anyway. He would undoubtedly be sick all over the kitchen floor. Victor was now standing looking up at Mrs Bone as if he was drinking in every word she said.

She ran out of breath at that point and there was a sudden silence. She was quite right, however – funny how often she was, thought Garth. Victor *was* sick.

This sight greatly improved Mrs Bone's temper, strangely enough. She was pleased at being right and even felt sorry for him.

He flapped his wings, which were about seven inches wide, and hung his head dismally.

'Poor love,' she said, even going so far as to pat it gingerly on the head. 'It's like stuffing a baby full of sausage and chips when it wants a nice bottle of milk.'

After a few days they began to find out what suited Victor. He wasn't a fussy bird. He always did his best to eat whatever was put in front of him, whether it suited him or not. What *really* suited him was milk, also honey and raw eggs. Every day, Mrs Bone boiled him up some bone broth. Sometimes he had a little chicken, sometimes minced beef loaf or Spam. He was a very trusting bird and nuzzled up to Garth whenever he fed him.

Although his beak and talons were as fearsome as an eagle's, Victor was in fact a gentle bird.

Indeed he did not have the haughty and rather cruel look that an eagle has.

Chapter Four

Soon it was the holidays and Robert often came to play with him and help feed Victor.

As the bird grew bigger, he ate more and more, and his beak became even more curved and shiny. His talons grew longer and sharper. His wings reached a width of nine inches across.

'You see,' Garth said to Robert one day, 'he uses his wings a lot – not only to fly with. When he's wet, he uses them as a towel to dry himself and when he's hot, he uses them as a fan.'

Victor stood between them as they

spoke ... His wings were slightly stretched like a cape, which made him look like a little old man as he gazed from Garth to Robert and back again as if he were following the conversation.

'My stars!' screeched his mother. 'You'd think he could talk!'

During the next few weeks, as Victor grew older, he became stronger and heavier. When he first came, Garth had enjoyed picking him up to put him in the rabbit-hutch at night. Now, he let Victor jump in by himself. He was a good bird and never objected to being put to bed at night.

He could fly much better too, swooping and curving and plummeting up and down and round and round. Sometimes, he went so high up that he was a mere dot in the sky.

Cats were afraid of him, while dogs barked at him from a safe distance. Only

one dog did not bark at him. This was Zebedee, a black Labrador. He snuffled through the fence at Victor and Victor calmly flapped his wings in reply. Then they sat down, either side of the fence, like two old friends. Zebedee usually came by two or three times a week now.

Little sparrows and blackbirds and thrushes took very little notice of him as long as he did not come too close to them. Most people around, when they heard about Victor, came to have a look at him.

They made various comments:

'Don't like the look of 'im' and

'Cor! Bet 'e eats a lot!' and

'Feeds on corpses, them do' and

'Not my idea of a pet' and (the one favourable comment),

'Happy-looking soul, in't he?'

They marvelled and then forgot all about him. If the Bones wanted to keep a

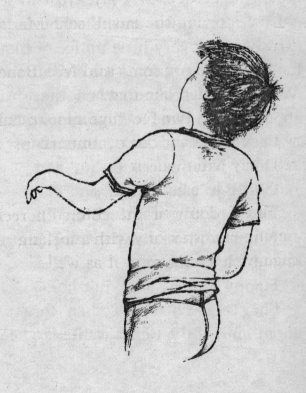

vulture in a rabbit-hutch as a pet, that was up to them.

Forgot about him, that is, until Councillor Dobbs came round at the end of August to judge the best-kept council gardens. You didn't have to enter for the competition – they looked at all the gardens anyway. 'Just to see if you're mowing the lawn,' said Mr Bone darkly.

'It's a free country,' said Mrs Bone. 'I like the garden like that.'

'That' was two feet high grass mingled with dock, dandelions, buttercups and rose bay willow herb.

'So do I,' said Garth.

'But I doubt if the council'll reckon much to it, especially with a socking great cage with a vulture in it as well.'

Chapter Five

Councillor Dobbs was a short man with an almost bald head. He wore a pin-stripe suit and a brown tie. His face was pink with little red veins when you saw him close to. Behind his glasses, his eyes looked remote, like pearls on the sea-bed.

He frowned when he saw the Bones' garden. He liked everything neat and tidy. There were too many animals rampaging around here. Anyone would think it was a private estate.

When he saw Victor, he was very

shocked indeed. If he'd had any hair it would have stood on end.

Everyone but Garth was out when he came. He was busy feeding Victor, when he saw the horrified face peering over the fence.

'Hello young man,' he said importantly. 'I'm Councillor Dobbs. What's that bird you've got there?'

'It's a vulture,' said Garth shortly. He didn't like being called 'young man'.

'I see. I didn't know there were any left in this country. Where did you get it?'

'Dad won it in a raffle.'

'In a raffle?' exclaimed Councillor Dobbs.

Victor walked clumsily over to him on his five-clawed feet. Councillor Dobbs jumped back nervously.

A sudden thought struck him and he

went quite pale. 'Let me see, this is No. 7 Ronaldsway, isn't it?' He noted it down in a little book and then hurried off, forgetting to say something about the garden as he had intended.

'Don't see what it's got to do wi' 'im,' said Mr Bone, when Garth told him. 'Why shouldn't I win it in a raffle?'

'I knew that bird would bring trouble,' said Mrs Bone. 'I knew it!'

'Fellow raffling it,' said Mr Bone, 'keeps a small garden of animals like at the back of his pub – not the "Red Cat" – one over the other side of Hatherton. Anyway, he's got some pheasants, a peacock, a fox and suchlike and this vulture. Turned out this vulture hatched a young 'un. Reckoned he couldn't afford to keep it as well as the mother so he raffled it.'

'The poor wee bird!' said Mrs Bone.

'I doubt that's the last we hear of it,' said Mr Bone, 'not if I know that old nosey-parker Dobbs.'

He was right, as the very next copy of the local paper showed.

'Just look at that!' said Mrs Bone, a week later, showing her husband a copy.

On the front page was a big black headline: COUNCIL HOUSE PETS ENQUIRY.

'In the council meeting, on Thursday, Councillor Dobbs drew the attention of the council to the matter of council house pets. Was the Chairman aware, he enquired, that vultures were being kept as pets, not half a mile away from that very chamber? Since, as far as he was aware, vultures were not indigenous to the British Isles ("Trust old Dobbs to use twenty words where six would do," muttered Mr Bone), it had probably been brought in from abroad. In view of the recent rabies scare, would the Chairman not consider taking the step of keeping a closer watch on pets in general?'

'Anyway,' said Mrs Bone, 'he's caused a lot of fuss and now they want to know where we got him from in case he's diseased. Diseased! The very idea! Just because we live in a council house, we're not capable of looking after our pets, I suppose!'

'There's a lot more too,' said Mr Bone, 'about corpses and a danger to children and all that rubbish.'

Garth was worried. 'They won't stop me keeping him, will they Dad?' he asked.

'Nay, lad, not if I've owt to do wi' it.'

'You're right,' said his mother fiercely. 'I must say I took against Victor when I first saw him but he's not been a bit of trouble, not a bit. And he's a right friendly bird too.'

Chapter Six

Sure enough, someone from the Council came round ('unofficial, like,' he said) to enquire about Victor. Mrs Bone invited him in and gave him a cup of tea and a slice of her home-baked Victoria sponge. Then she explained that Victor had not been smuggled in from abroad or anything like that and told him the whole story.

Then Mr Jones, for that was his name, watched out of the kitchen window while Garth fed him. Mr Jones went away very impressed with Garth, Victor and Mrs Bone's cooking.

The next visitor Mrs Bone had was Mrs Porker from a house near by.

She didn't look a bit like a pig despite her name. She was small and bird-like with white hair.

'This is only the thin end of the wedge,' she said fiercely to Mrs Bone. 'The thin end of the wedge. They can't tell us what pets we can keep. At that rate they'll stop us keeping any at all soon. That Dobbs man's trying to frighten everyone by talking about rabies.' Mrs Porker had a Pyrenean mountain dog and a tabby cat. 'We must get up a petition,' she said firmly, 'and ask everyone to sign it.'

'What's a petition?' asked Garth.

'It's a sort of request,' said Mrs Porker. 'We write a letter to the council about the pets we keep, say how well we look after them and all that sort of thing,

and demand that the liberty to keep pets should not be taken away from us. Then we try to get everyone or as many people as possible to sign it. Then we present it to the Council.'

'Oh,' said Garth.

'Good idea,' said Mrs Bone. 'Why don't you write it out, Alice? Then we'll sign it.'

Mrs Porker looked pleased. 'Right you are,' she said. Off she went, promising to get it done as soon as possible and muttering again about it being 'the thin end of the wedge'.

There were a lot of people on the estate as it was divided up into lots of separate parts, named after airports. Garth lived in Ronaldsway. Next to these were Gatwick, Heathrow, Lungi and Nairobi. And right at the top were two older estates which had chimneys and coal-fires instead of central heating.

These were called Coronation Avenue and Jubilee Road.

Mrs Porker was soon busily trotting round the estate with her petition. 'When I've tried a few houses,' she explained to Garth, who was accompanying her so that he could write down all the people who refused (with reasons), or the number of houses where there was no one at home, 'I'll get more idea what people feel about it.'

The first house they visited was Mrs Porker's neighbour. Since she came to the door holding a fat black cat, Garth knew she would sign it. The housewife in the next house was obviously busy.

'Do I have to pay anything?' she asked and when Mrs Porker assured her that she didn't, she signed it without reading it.

Garth thought that was silly. In stories, she would have signed away her

life or her fortune, but evidently she did not read that sort of story.

'Well, I don't know that I approve of vultures,' said the next man, winking at Garth, 'but I don't see why we should be harassed by the Council.' (He was a darts friend of Mr Bone.)

Mrs Porker was very pleased. 'I think most people will sign it,' she said. 'Even some of those who don't have pets them-selves will if they're reasonable. Most people don't object to other people having pets even if they don't want them.'

She was right. Several people without pets signed it and, even stranger, Garth thought, some with pets didn't.

'Some people don't like signing any-thing,' explained Mrs Porker. 'And others again think their cat or rabbit or gerbil is all right but not your vulture, for instance, or my dog. As they say round here, "there's nowt so queer as folk".'

Over the next week, they collected an impressive list of signatures.

At last, when they'd called at every house at least once and some two or three times, they had enough signatures.

'Now I have to send it to someone at the Town Hall and await results,' said Mrs Porker.

Chapter Seven

Meanwhile Mrs Bone was getting worried about the amount of food Victor consumed. 'There they are in the shops,' she said to her husband, 'complaining about the price of food. Moaning about the price of bread and suchlike – well it is dear, now I remember when I was a girl it was sixpence a loaf – anyway I was saying how much it cost us to feed our bird and they all laughed. They said well a budgie doesn't eat much. A budgie! I ask you! All the same, love, it's no joke feeding that vulture, you know. It's getting more expensive all the time.'

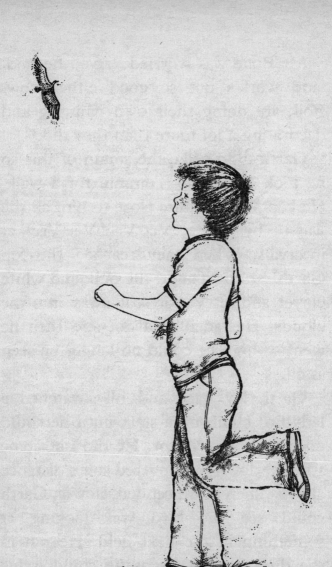

Mr Bone was worried. 'Aye,' he said, 'and work's not so good either now. Folk are doing their own painting and decorating a lot more than they did.'

Garth didn't like the sound of this so he took Victor up Tommul for a walk. He kept Victor quite close to him all the way up by calling, 'Vee Vee! Vee Vee!' at intervals. When they reached the top Garth sat down amid the pink and white clover and let Victor soar away into the clouds. He faded to a dot and then he went so high he could no longer be seen at all.

Garth lay back and idly watched a ladybird climb up a stalk until he could once more see Victor. He did not come straight down but hovered some distance above. Then he descended, slowly. Garth could see the bird was looking at something in the next field. He ran in the direction, as far as he could judge it, of Victor's gaze. At last he saw. A lamb had fallen down a steep bank and lay feebly on its back near a sluggishly trickling stream. Probably it had wandered away from the flock and had then hurt a leg in falling down the bank. It bleated feebly, its eyes half-closed.

Victor alighted beside Garth on the grass. 'Come on Vee Vee,' said Garth. 'We'll call at the farmhouse and tell Mr Butlin about it.' Victor hopped and flew along beside him. Mr Butlin was in the farmyard, talking to one of his labourers. A strong smell of dung, sweat and hawthorn filled Garth's nostrils.

'What's oop?' asked the labourer.

Garth quickly explained about the lamb. The farmer frowned. 'They shouldna be in thet field there, by rights. There's a hole in the fence, 'appen. See to 'un, Joe. I'll see to the lamb.'

Garth (and Victor) walked back with

him to show him the way. As the farmer paused to knock the dirt off his wellington boots, he took a look at the vulture. 'Your pet that?' he asked abruptly.

'Yes,' said Garth. 'He's a vulture. I saw him looking at something and that's how I found the lamb.'

'Ah!' said Mr Butlin. 'I didn't think he was a penguin like.'

They reached the lamb and Mr Butlin slished down the dry, dusty bank in his wellingtons and gently picked it up.

'It'll do,' he said, looking at it carefully, 'though I daresay it's broke its leg. We'll need to keep it in the kitchen like for a while. Lucky we found it though. Thank you, lad.'

Garth ran off, seeing he was no longer required, and reached home to find his mother scanning the green for him.

'Oh!' she said. 'So you're back, are

you? I thought that daft bird had carried you off!' Garth told her all about the lamb. She didn't look pleased or say how clever Victor was. She looked worried.

Chapter Eight

A few weeks later, Mrs Porker reported that the matter was going to be discussed in that night's council meeting. 'I'm going along to hear what they've got to say,' she said. 'They've got the petition.'

'Can I come?' asked Garth.

'Of course,' said Mrs Porker. 'Anyone can.'

The Town Hall was opposite an old cinema which now showed only Indian and Pakistani films on Thursdays and Saturdays. As it was Thursday night, the council chamber windows were closed although it was very hot. Otherwise

occasional loud bursts of oriental music would be heard in the chamber. Mrs Porker and Garth arrived early before the councillors and council officers. Large shiny-looking mahogany desks, behind which stood armchairs seated in green leather, took up most of the space. At the front of the room on the right side of Garth was a platform. On it were three chairs.

' 'That's where the Mayor used to sit when they had one,' said Mrs Porker, 'and the Deputy-Mayor. Right shame that is. Everything's new-fangled these days. They've done away with the Mayor – said he was old-fashioned and spent too much money. So now they've a Chairman instead. She uses the very same car the Mayor used and wears the same chain so I don't see the difference.' She stopped talking as the councillors began to wander into the chamber.

'Who's the other man on the platform with the red nose?' asked Garth.

'That's the Chief Executive Officer,' said Mrs Porker. Soon all the councillors who were coming had arrived and it was time for the meeting to start. Garth found it very boring at first. He had begun to doze off in the close atmosphere when suddenly Mrs Porker nudged him. Someone was reading out the petition. Garth sat up and began to listen carefully. It appeared that each of the fifty-one members of the District Council had something to say on the matter and was determined to say it. The nuisance of stray dogs was discussed, the distressing noise made by courting cats, the prolific breeding of rabbits and all sorts of other animal ways displeasing to humans while, on the other hand, the useful purpose they served as friends, companions, rat-killers, protectors, etc. was also mentioned. All the time Mrs Porker became angrier and angrier. 'None of this is anything to do with it,' she whispered to Garth. 'It's whether we, as council tenants, have the same rights to keep animals as other people.' At last someone got up and made this very point which set everybody off again. It was certainly agreed by most of the members that it was a terrible thing if people were not allowed to keep pets but, as Councillor Dobbs was quick to point out, there must be some kind of a limit on what could reasonably be regarded as a pet. 'Otherwise,' he finished amid laughter, 'we shall be getting requests for pet gorillas, hyenas and even sabre-toothed tigers. I don't, in all conscience, ladies and gentlemen, think a vulture can be included in the same category as a rabbit or a Scottie dog.'

'Oh dear!' said Mrs Porker. Garth bit his lip and then stood up before anyone else could say anything.

'My vulture,' he began amid gasps of astonishment, 'is very friendly and very intelligent. He's always lived with people. I don't think he'd like to go any-where else now. He was born in captivity and he likes people. He even rescued a sheep for Mr Butlin who has a farm over Tommul. I don't know why people are so prejudiced against vultures.' His voice cracked on the last word and he sat down quickly to prevent himself crying. There was a hum of conversation and the Chairman had to bang on the table with her spectacle-case for silence.

'Although, strictly speaking, you are not allowed to speak at a council meeting, I'm sure we were all very impressed with what you had to say.' There were cries of

'Hear Hear!' and 'Which party were you thinking of joining, lad?'

She smiled at Garth. 'I'm sure you are very attached to your vulture. This does you great credit. I think, fellow members, this is something we can more usefully discuss in committee with Garth and his parents, isn't it, and not something to be ruled in a full meeting of the Council?'

With that Mrs Porker and Garth went home but not before they had been snapped by a reporter from the local paper. He took down Garth's address as well and asked if he could come round and snap Victor. Garth was too miserable to care. He went silently home. What would become of Victor without him? Would they take him back where he'd come from? No, he remembered. They couldn't – he wasn't wanted or he wouldn't have been raffled in the first

place. Would they put him ... no they couldn't do that – he refused even to think it. What would they do then? He didn't believe they would let him keep Victor. He tossed and turned half the night, thinking about it. He finally fell asleep to dream that he went to school to find behind the teacher's desk, not Miss Molesley, but Councillor Dobbs. Behind each of the desks in the classroom sat, not children, but twenty-nine vultures. When he walked to his usual seat, they all flew towards him, menacingly. He woke up shouting to a bright sunny day and Victor waiting patiently to be fed.

Chapter Nine

Well! The Bone family had never known such excitement as in the next few days after the council meeting. Garth's picture was in the paper and so was Victor's, of course. So also was Farmer Butlin. The whole story of the lamb was re-told. Garth didn't care a jot. He just worried about what was going to happen to Victor.

The Sunday after the meeting, a long black Mercedes-Benz rolled up to the Bones' house. It was the Chairman's official car. She wasn't wearing her chain of office though, Garth saw, as she stepped out of the car. She wore a bright

yellow dress and a white hat. Mrs Bone was rather surprised and got out her best china tea-service with the blue roses on it. Mr Bone, afraid that someone would come and photograph the garden, was at long last mowing it with Mrs Porker's mower.

The Chairman beamed at Garth and his mother as she sipped the tea out of Mrs Bone's best teacup and tasted her freshly baked treacle tart.

'Mm. Delicious,' she said. 'Now, I've got an idea. I know Garth is fond of his bird and I'm also sure that he must be costing a very great deal to keep.'

'He certainly does,' cried Mrs Bone. 'Most often these days it seems as if he's hungry.' She told the Chairman all the things Victor liked eating.

'I wonder,' said the Chairman, 'whether you would like to keep him as a pet, Garth, but would let him live elsewhere?'

'Whatever do you mean?' asked Mrs Bone. 'Not live here but still be his pet?'

'Well,' said the Chairman. 'What about the Animal Corner in the Park?'

Garth knew it well. There were white rabbits, goats, a peacock and a variety of swans and ducks. He often went there to look at the whooper swan which was his favourite.

'Oh!' he said. 'You mean Victor could live there.'

'Yes!' said the Chairman. 'He would be a great attraction. The park authorities would be responsible for feeding him, of course, but he would still be yours.'

Garth returned to hope from the pit of despair he had been floundering in. He felt suddenly light-hearted, light-headed. He began to whistle.

'It would be marvellous not having to feed him,' said his mother. 'We could afford a Sunday joint again.'

Garth could scarcely get used to the idea that Victor was safe – he was not going to be killed or sent away somewhere where they would never see each other again.

'Would I be able to take him out for a fly sometimes?' he asked. 'You see he's used to me now and he always comes back again.'

'I'm sure that could be arranged,' she said. 'After all, he's yours. And I think Victor would enjoy people coming to look at him, don't you?'

That weekend, when everything had been arranged, Garth took Victor down to the park. There he met Heck, a big burly man who was in charge of all the animals and birds.

He took to Victor at once.

Victor soon settled down happily there. Every evening Garth strolled down to the park and took him out for a fly, and at weekends he always helped to feed him.

When they went back to school, Garth was in the top Juniors. He didn't have Miss Molesley any more as his teacher.

He had a new teacher. She was called Mrs Morton. She was short and plump with dark hair.

'Now children,' she said, on the first day of term, 'I don't know any of you yet so I want you to write about yourselves for me. *Today* I want you to write about your pets.'

'Cardboard porridge!' groaned Robert. 'She's just like Miss Molesley. Composition all the time.'

But Garth didn't mind. In fact he'd already started his.

'I have a pet called Victor,' he began. 'He is a griffon vulture and lives in the "Animal Corner" in the park.' For once he was going to write something better than Delia Greenwood. He chewed the end of his pen: he was content.